Note to parents, carers and teachers

Read it yourself is a series of modern stories, favourite characters and traditional tales written in a simple way for children who are learning to read. The books can be read independently or as part of a guided reading session.

Each book is carefully structured to include many high-frequency words vital for first reading. The sentences on each page are supported closely by pictures to help with understanding, and to offer lively details to talk about.

The books are graded into four levels that progressively introduce wider vocabulary and longer stories as a reader's ability and confidence grows.

Ideas for use

- Begin by looking through the book and talking about the pictures. Has your child heard this story before?

- Help your child with any words he does not know, either by helping him to sound them out or supplying them yourself.

- Developing readers can be concentrating so hard on the words that they sometimes don't fully grasp the meaning of what they're reading. Answering the puzzle questions on pages 30 and 31 will help with understanding.

For more information and advice on Read it yourself and book banding, visit **www.ladybird.com/readityourself**

Book
Band
5

Level 1 is ideal for children who have received some initial reading instruction. Each story is told very simply, using a small number of frequently repeated words.

Special features:

stepmother

Opening pages introduce key story words

fairy godmother

first stepsister

second stepsister

shoe

Cinderella

6

7

Careful match between story and pictures

Cinderella lived with her stepmother and stepsisters.
Cinderella's stepmother and stepsisters made Cinderella clean the house.

Large, clear type

8

9

Educational Consultant: Geraldine Taylor
Book Banding Consultant: Kate Ruttle

A catalogue record for this book is available from the British Library

Published by Ladybird Books Ltd
80 Strand, London, WC2R 0RL
A Penguin Company

006

ISBN: 978-0-72327-267-0

Printed in China

Cinderella

Illustrated by Marina Le Ray

first
stepsister

second
stepsister

stepmother

castle

fairy godmother

shoe

Cinderella

Cinderella lived with her stepmother and stepsisters.

Cinderella's stepmother and stepsisters made Cinderella clean the house.

One day, there was a ball
at the castle.

"Can I go to the ball?"
said Cinderella.
"No," said her stepsisters.

"You do not have a dress," said the first stepsister.

"You do not have any shoes," said the second stepsister.

A fairy godmother came to Cinderella's house.

She made Cinderella a beautiful dress and some beautiful shoes.

Cinderella put on her beautiful dress. She put on her beautiful shoes. "Now I can go to the ball," she said.

The prince danced
with Cinderella.

After the ball, the prince
found Cinderella's shoe.

"I will marry the girl who will fit this shoe," he said.

The prince came to Cinderella's house.

"Is this your shoe?" he said.

"Yes, this is my shoe," said the first stepsister.

But the shoe did not fit.

"Is this your shoe?" said
the prince.
"Yes, this is my shoe,"
said the second stepsister.
But the shoe did not fit.

"Is this your shoe?"
said the prince.

"Yes," said Cinderella.
She put on the shoe
and it fit.

"Will you marry me?"
said the prince.

"Yes," said Cinderella.

So she did!

How much do you remember about the story of Cinderella? Answer these questions and find out!

- Who does Cinderella live with?

- What does the fairy godmother make for Cinderella to wear?

- How does the prince find Cinderella after the ball?

Look at the pictures from the story and say the order they should go in.

A

B

C

D

Read it yourself with Ladybird

Tick the books you've read!

For children who are ready to take their first steps in reading.

Level 1

The Enormous Turnip

Fairy Friends

Goldilocks and the Three Bears

Little Red Hen

The Magic Porridge Pot

Little Creatures

Recycling Fun!

The Princess and the Pea

Cinderella

Rex the Big Dinosaur

The Tale of Peter Rabbit

The Three Billy Goats Gruff

Why Giraffe has a Long Neck

Go to the Zoo

The Ugly Duckling

The Emperor's New Clothes

For beginner readers who can read short, simple sentences with help.

Level 2

Beauty and the Beast

Chicken Licken

Little Red Riding Hood

Nature Trail

Sports Day

Pirate School

Rumpelstiltskin

Sleeping Beauty

The Gingerbread Man

Sly Fox and Red Hen

The Tale of Jemima Puddle-Duck

The Three Little Pigs

Why Lion Roarrrs!

The Big Race

Town Mouse Country Mouse

Dan's Dragon

The Read it yourself with Ladybird app is now available for iPad, iPhone and iPod touch

App also available on Android devices